DATE DUE

JAN 2 5 1999			
APR 2 0 2002			
AUG 0 7 2010			
SEP 2 3 2011			

A Message from
the Match Girl

A Richard Jackson Book

INVESTIGATORS OF THE UNKNOWN
BOOK THREE

A Message from the Match Girl

JANET TAYLOR LISLE

Orchard Books • New York

Orchard Books
95 Madison Avenue, New York, NY 10016

Manufactured in the United States of America
Book design by Mina Greenstein
The text of this book is set in 12 point New Aster.
3   5   7   9   10   8   6   4

Library of Congress Cataloging-in-Publication Data
Lisle, Janet Taylor.
A message from the match girl / Janet Taylor Lisle.
p.   cm.—(Investigators of the unknown ; bk. 3)
"A Richard Jackson book."
Summary: Georgina and Poco try to help their
friend Walter who is suffering from an identity
crisis and receiving strange messages from his dead
mother.
ISBN 0-531-09487-1.   ISBN 0-531-08787-5 (lib. bdg.)
[1. Supernatural—Fiction.   2. Friendship—
Fiction.   3. Identity—Fiction.   4. Orphans—
Fiction.   5. Mothers and sons—Fiction.]
I. Title.   II. Series: Lisle, Janet
Taylor.   Investigators of the unknown ; bk. 3.
PZ7.L6912Me   1995
[Fic]—dc20   95-6036

A Message from
the Match Girl

ONE

At first, Walter Kew hardly knew he was being haunted. His mother's voice came so softly, like a thought that might have been his own. He would be walking home from school or slouching on the front steps of his house, and the wind would ruffle his hair like an invisible hand. Then he would hear her.

Not "Hello, Walter, how are you doing down there on earth?" Or "It's been a while since I've seen you, dear. Are you remembering to brush your teeth?"

Walter's mother didn't talk like other mothers. She had died nine years ago when he was a baby, so her words had to travel across dark oceans of time. When they finally reached Walter, they were as faint and uncertain as ghosts.

She spoke in tones that Walter sensed more than heard. He would sit perfectly still, head cocked to one side, and her voice would come whispering into his mind. Then it drifted off before he quite caught her meaning, and nothing he did would bring her back again. He was sure of one thing. She wanted to tell him something.

"How do you know?" Walter's friend Georgina Rusk asked him. "How do you even know it's your mother? You can't remember what her voice sounded like. You were too little when she died to remember anything about her. This voice could be anyone's, from anywhere. Or maybe it's no one's and you're making it up." She gave him a narrow glance.

Walter pulled his baseball cap down low over his eyes. "I know it's my mother," he said. "People don't make mistakes about things like mothers."

"Since when?" asked Georgina. "They're like everyone else."

"No they aren't. You don't know. You see yours every day. All these years I've been trying to get through to mine. I've tried spells and dreams and crystal balls. Even when I asked the Ouija board, I was never sure I got her. Now, at last, she's making contact with me—except there's some kind of interference on the line."

"Interference! What is this, a credit card call?"

Walter sighed and took off his cap. Georgina's mind was of the practical, earthbound sort. Unknown things like ghosts were too shadowy for her. As for ghost voices trying to get through—

"You mean dirt interference?" she asked him, suddenly serious. "From your mother being, you know, buried underground?"

"Not dirt. Something outside this world." Walter's eyes flicked away. They were the palest blue, almost white in certain lights. "Spirit-seeing eyes," their friend Poco Lambert called them. At school, teachers snapped their fingers under his nose: "Control tower to Walter! Please come in!"

"It's an ages-old communication problem," he

informed Georgina now. "I'm not the only one who's had trouble. Only a few people in history have ever heard what the dead were trying to tell them."

"That is certainly okay with me," Georgina said. "Who needs a lot of ghosts calling up and telling you things? There are enough living people trying to do that already. . . . Nothing against your mother," she added quickly. "I'm sure she was a very nice person."

"But that's the whole point. She still is!" Walter cried. "My mother's still out there, and now she wants to come back."

Two

"WALTER'S MIND isn't right," Georgina said to Poco as the two walked toward the park on Saturday morning. "I think he's made up this ghost because he misses his mom. It's sort of sad. I never know what to say."

"Just look interested," Poco advised. "There might be more to it."

She was small and precise, but no one had ever accused her of being earthbound. Poco could detect the unknown at work in a blade of grass, not to mention birds and squirrels, with whom she regularly spoke.

"Walter has special antennae that pick up invisible signals," she told Georgina now. "That's why he acts so strange sometimes. Have you seen how his eyes suddenly lock open and he doesn't hear when you speak to him?"

"Everyone's seen that. What's going on?"

"He's watching out." Poco raised her own head and gazed at the sky. "He's checking ahead and looking behind. There are worlds out there that only Walter sees, and they aren't exactly the safest places. If your parents had died and there was just one old grandmother left to take care of you, you might have had to grow special antennae, too."

"Not me," said Georgina, kicking a stone out of her path. "I'd have bought double locks and a burglar alarm."

It was April, but the weather was still cold. Too cold, really, for a visit to the park. The friends would never have thought of going there if Walter had not phoned them the night before.

"I have something to show you," he'd said in his cautious way. "In the park . . . if you want to see it."

"Of course we want to see it!" Georgina had bellowed.

He was the sort of person who never gave orders, who never asked for anything and waited until the cookies were passed before taking one. Mothers loved him. He was so quiet and polite. They couldn't resist patting his head, cap and all. Georgina's mother was always asking him for lunch, though he rarely came. Quietly, politely, he'd say he had to go home.

But children his own age didn't have time for quietness, and politeness was seen as giving in to the enemy. At school, he was mostly shoved aside. Only those who looked closely could see how he minded.

"Have you noticed how Walter never talks about his father?" Georgina said to Poco as they walked along. "His mother wasn't the only one who got killed. Both his parents died in that terrible accident."

"What happened anyway? No one ever said."

"He's never told. Lucky his grandparents could take him in. Otherwise Walter might have had to be an orphan."

"He *is* an orphan." Poco examined the sky again. "That's what you are when your parents are dead. I guess Walter's father isn't the one haunting him. Walter thinks about him. He's just got to find out what his mother wants first."

"How could she want anything? She's been dead for nine years!"

"She might have decided to come back and fix a wrong. The dead come back if they feel guilty."

"Oh, sure." Georgina snorted under her breath. But no sooner had she said this than an icy finger of wind slipped down her spine and she jumped and looked about uneasily.

Poco didn't notice. She was checking her pockets. In the left one, she felt the package of crackers that she had remembered to bring for the poor cold ducks in the park's pond. "So they won't stare at us with their hungry duck eyes," she'd explained.

"Only you could feel sorry for ducks!" Georgina had blustered.

There was also, in her right pocket, a small plastic bag of birdseed, in case someone interesting should happen to flap by. In particular, Poco was on the lookout for a robin she'd met last winter. He hadn't come around lately and, as they walked, she kept glancing worriedly at the sky.

"I know you're watching for that idiot robin,"

Georgina said. "I hope you aren't going to start talking to him again if he shows up. It's terribly embarrassing to normal people like me."

"Georgina! You are so prejudiced." Poco shook her head. "This robin is a very intelligent bird. You should never judge a person only by his feathers. And there's Walter," she added, cutting off the next protest. "Come on, let's run."

He was standing on a small rise at the far edge of the grassy clearing that formed the park—Andersen Park, as it was named, in honor of the great storyteller Hans Christian Andersen. A hundred years ago a rich family had given this land to the town. Wanting it to be a proper place for children, they had commissioned a series of bronze statues in the shape of characters from Andersen's most famous tales.

As Poco and Georgina ran toward Walter, they skirted a large model of the Ugly Duckling, frozen in mid-waddle near the edge of the pond. In a meadow to one side, Thumbelina danced stiffly on a swallow's back. A sharp-nosed Steadfast Tin Soldier stood at attention near the park gates. In the swings area the Snow Queen surveyed the sandbox through flat, weather-worn eyes.

Posed motionless above this strange collection, Walter looked almost like a statue himself. He was gazing down at something in his hand. When Poco and Georgina came up, he stuffed it in his pocket.

"Well?" panted Georgina. "Aren't you going to say hello?"

"Hello," Walter said in an uncertain tone.

"Aren't you supposed to show us something?" Georgina demanded. "We didn't walk all this way to stand around doing nothing!"

Under his baseball cap, Walter's pale eyes grew paler. Georgina always scared him a little. He turned toward Poco for help, but she happened to be looking just then at the sky.

"He's around here somewhere," she was muttering. "He told me once he hangs out in the park on Saturdays. He's a friendly type and doesn't mind crowds."

"Walter!" cried Georgina, who often felt she was the only sensible person in the group. "You've got something in your pocket. You're going to show it to us, right? Is it about your mother?"

He nodded.

"I thought so. You found a note she wrote

before she died, explaining everything about her and your dad?"

Walter shook his head sadly.

"Your mother left you something in her will, and your grandmother finally remembered to give it to you?"

"Sort of. Without the will." Walter glanced over his shoulder. Behind him, in the shadow of some trees, stood another Hans Christian Andersen statue. It was the Little Match Girl, half-huddled on the ground. She wore a ragged dress with wide front pockets, and a patched shawl over her shoulders. Her small bronze face was turned a bit to one side as if she wished to shield it from some assault. Perhaps an icy wind? The Match Girl's story was one of abandonment in winter. Walter stared at her, then looked back at his friends.

"Last night my grandmother gave me a photograph." Poco's eyes were instantly on him. "She didn't want to. She said I was too young. I told her I couldn't stand it anymore. I had to know something about my parents. I said it was strange there was nothing left behind. Not even any pictures."

"It's more than strange," Georgina said. "It's suspicious. People don't just die and disappear without a trace. Didn't they ever write letters?"

Walter shrugged. "My grandmother's so old. She says she can't remember. But suddenly, last night, she remembered this photo."

He reached into his pocket and drew it out, holding the edges with the tips of his fingers. "It's of me and my mother. The first picture of her I've ever seen."

Georgina and Poco came around to stand beside him. The photo was in color, but faded.

"You look as if you were just born," Poco said.

"I think I was. It's winter in the picture. My birthday's in September."

"I can't see your mother very well. Is that her back?" Georgina asked.

"Yes." Walter sucked in his breath. "Isn't it . . . amazing?"

Actually, the photo seemed very ordinary to Poco and Georgina. Though they dared not say so, it was the sort of picture that would certainly have been thrown away if a person were picking and choosing. It showed so little. In the foreground there was the shoulder of a plain cloth coat and the back of a woman's head, dark and curly haired. Over her shoulder a baby's face looked out from a bundle of blankets. The baby's eyes were pale and gazed inquisitively toward the camera. One small arm was flung forward, showing a mitten attached by button to a tiny sleeve. The rest of the baby's body was hidden. So was every bit of the woman's face.

"I can see it's you, Walter, because of your eyes," Poco said. "Too bad your mother didn't turn around."

"She looks like she's turning away on purpose. Maybe she didn't want to be seen," Georgina said. "What's that behind her?"

Poco bent closer. "It's—" She gasped. "It's the Little Match Girl! This picture was taken here!"

Walter nodded. "That's why you had to come. Look, the trees are bigger now, but they're the same as in the photo. And there's the same grass and the same clump of bushes. In fact, my mother was standing exactly on this spot when she . . . I mean when we . . ."

An odd little choke came from his throat. He turned toward the frozen figure behind him. Georgina and Poco turned around, too. All three stared at the sad little girl, who seemed suddenly more real and closer to them than before.

"If only she could speak and tell us what she knows," Walter said. "She was here. She saw everything." For a moment he seemed about to reach out and touch her.

"Maybe she will," Poco murmured. "Maybe, in a way, she's already begun."

THREE

DIRECTLY ACROSS from the entrance to Andersen Park was a well-known sandwich shop and snack place. It had stood there for many years, selling sandwiches to people on their lunch breaks, and ice cream to families spending the day in the park. Now, as the friends walked out through the park gate, it caught their attention. A minute later, after some prodding from Georgina, they agreed to go in and get something to eat.

"You are looking a little weak in the knees,"

Poco said to Walter. "And since Georgina has so nicely offered to pay—"

"I did not!" cried Georgina, who meant to be generous but always had second thoughts when the moment came. "I said I had some money with me, that's all. You both have to pay me back later!" She caught sight of a red-faced old man glaring at her from behind a meat counter and blushed.

"In that case, Walter and I will have something huge and delicious," Poco announced. "If we have to pay later anyway, we might as well have the best!"

Poco looked small and shy, but she could speak up when the moment called for it. Georgina, on the other hand, tended to hang back in public places, even after she had pushed others into them. There was always the danger that she would make a fool of herself. While Poco read the menu with Walter, she peeked around to see if the old man was still watching. With relief, she saw that he had disappeared. A door to the store's back room was still swinging.

"How about a hot fudge sundae, Walter?" Poco asked. "I'm going to get one and order extra nuts. I don't really like nuts on sundaes, but I'm friends with a family that wouldn't mind a delivery. It's been a long, hard winter in the squirrel world."

A wispy-haired waitress appeared at their table, pad in hand.

"Three hot fudge sundaes, please. All with extra nuts," Poco said. Her friends seemed unable to speak for themselves. Walter had pulled his cap far down over his eyes, as if he might be trying to tune in to his mother.

Georgina, meanwhile, was having an attack of nerves. She had suddenly remembered that she'd never before been in a restaurant without her parents. Was she old enough to pay the check? Would the red-faced man shout at her and throw her out? He had not looked like a pleasant person. Even the waitress seemed to be afraid. She kept glancing toward the back room while she made their sundaes.

Walter took out the photograph of his mother and stared at it again.

"Do you have any memory of her now?" Poco asked him. "I was wondering if the picture might have brought something back."

He shook his head. "I don't remember anything. Not about my father or the terrible accident either. As far as I know, I was always with my grandparents. Then my grandfather died and there was just me and Granny."

"Could your father have taken the picture?" Poco asked.

Walter gazed at her with his pale, haunted eyes. "I didn't think of that."

"I guess there's no way to know for sure."

"But it could be true. Maybe my mother wasn't hiding her face. Maybe my father was trying to get in close to take a good shot of me, so she put me up on her shoulder to make it easier."

Poco nodded. "Maybe your parents decided to take you for a walk in the park. It was a cold winter day, so they bundled you up. Your dad brought his camera, but you were so little he couldn't get a clear shot. You couldn't even sit up by yourself yet. So he told your mother to turn around and . . ."

The waitress arrived with napkins and spoons and the hot fudge sundaes on a tray. They were big ones with streams of chocolate sauce pouring down the sides, and whipped cream on top.

"But where are the nuts?" Poco asked, when the sundaes had been set down. "You forgot to put them on."

Without saying a word, the waitress took

another bowl off her tray and put it on the table. It was filled with nuts.

"And here is a plastic bag and a twist," she murmured, bending close to Poco. "So you can carry the nuts to your squirrel friends, okay?" She tucked the bag into Poco's hand.

Poco was astonished. "How did you know?" she was about to ask, when the waitress raised a finger to her lips. She nodded toward the back room.

"Watch out," she whispered. "He would be angry if he knew."

"Thank you very much!" Poco whispered back.

The waitress smiled and stepped away.

"That was so nice," Poco whispered to the others. "I guess she heard us talking. Maybe she likes squirrels."

Walter shrugged. He wanted to go on with the story about his parents. He was frantic to go on. While Poco and Georgina dug into their sundaes, he began to tell them other reasons why his parents might have come to the park that day.

They were happy; no, they were sad. They were worried; no, they needed exercise. They had something important to talk about. They were just tired of being in the house. They met some friends. They walked alone. They took turns carrying him. When it started snowing, they caught snowflakes on their gloves and let him taste them. He was surprised by the flakes' coldness and began to cry, so they hugged him until he . . .

Georgina and Poco put their hands over their ears.

"Walter, stop!"

"We've heard enough."

"Can't we talk about something else?"

His feelings were hurt, and he turned to the window. The Little Match Girl statue was faintly visible through the park gates across the street. He stared in her direction during the rest of their time in the restaurant, forgetting even to eat his sundae.

Afterward he wanted to go alone to stand by the statue again, so Poco and Georgina agreed to wait for him. They threw Poco's crackers to the ducks in the pond and then sat patiently on the grass. This was very nice of them, considering how chilly it was. Walter didn't notice, though. In the distance they heard his voice rising and falling. They knew he was talking about his parents again, inventing more things they might have done on that long-ago day in the park.

"What is wrong with him?" Georgina demanded at last.

"He's hungry for stories," Poco said. "In fact, he's starving. It happened to some baby rabbits I met."

"Oh please."

"It's true. Their mother got eaten by a coyote, and they grew up never knowing who she was. So they used to sit around making things up. Sometimes they pretended she was a beautiful silver house rabbit, sometimes a famous jumping rabbit from the north. The other rabbits laughed, but they didn't care. They had to have stories just as much as food, otherwise they would have shriveled up and died."

"Good grief!" Georgina said. "You can't die from that."

"Yes you can," said Poco, who could be shockingly wise at times. "There are things you have to know. You have to know where you came from, or you can't go on. You have to have stories about yourself."

"Then why won't Walter's grandmother tell him?"

"I don't know," Poco said. "I think it means that something's wrong."

A nervous swan hissed at them. Poco's robin seemed to have flown somewhere else. Or maybe he was huddled in a nest. The wind was icy when it blew hard.

"I think that waitress really did care about squirrels," Poco remarked a little later. "She kept coming back and watching to make sure we took the nuts. When we left, I saw her spying on us from the back room."

"I think she was hoping we'd give her a big tip," Georgina said. "But I couldn't remember how much I should leave, so I didn't put anything down at all."

FOUR

WALTER KEW could not get used to having, in his pocket, a picture of his very own mother. He could not get used to taking the picture out and looking at it. It didn't matter that his mother's face was hidden. The back of her head was fine. More than fine, it was beautiful.

He looked at it in the mornings when he first woke up and at breakfast while he ate his cereal. He looked at it on the way to school, in the hall between classes, and during lunch. When school was over, he walked to the park, stood near the Little Match Girl, and stared at the photo. No one asked what he was doing there. He stood so still that he might as well have been invisible.

After dinner—which never lasted long, since there were only two at table, Walter and his grandmother—he carried the photo up to his room and held it under the desk lamp until the surface turned hot and sticky. This brought out mysterious shadows in the picture. He saw a dark shape reflected in the baby's eyes—in *his* eyes. Was it his father? Walter's heart beat faster.

At night, after his grandmother had tucked him in tight, the way he liked, after she had given him her shy, old-fashioned pat ("What a big boy you are now," she often murmured), Walter listened to her shoes clump away down the hall. Then a terrible loneliness would come creeping toward his bed. Like a hungry wolf, it would sniff at his shoulder, tug at the sheets. In fright, he would search his mind for a memory: a face, a color, a touch, a sound—anything to connect him to the woman in the photo.

There was nothing.

He would hold his breath and listen for his

mother's voice. "Please!" he would pray. Most nights it didn't come.

"She never comes when I need her," he told Poco. "And even when she does, I can't understand her."

"Give her time," Poco said. "Maybe she's working things out."

Time! Walter didn't have it. He began to show the photo to other people. To the soft-voiced art teacher at school. To the waitress in the sandwich shop across from the park, where he went to buy candy. The librarian in the public library smiled when he showed her.

"What a cutie," she said, taking the photo in her hand. "Is that your new baby brother?"

Walter had nodded. How else could he explain? Anyway, the baby did seem like a new brother. He was amazingly young and impossibly small, a person Walter might get to know if he stared hard enough.

He stared mostly at his mother's head. Sometimes he spoke to it in his room.

"Who are you?" he'd ask, right out loud. "Do you still love me?" Then he'd cover his mouth. What a stupid thing to say!

Only later he realized it wasn't that stupid. From across her dark ocean his ghost-mother must have heard, because not long afterward a message arrived. Eerily but fittingly, it came from the Little Match Girl.

GEORGINA LEAPT straight up in the air when she heard.

"A message?" she cried. "From the Match Girl? Where?"

"Right here," Walter said. While Georgina and Poco watched, he took from his back pocket an ordinary white envelope, rather bent from being pressed into chairs all day. Walter, being Walter, had waited until the very end of school to show them.

"Good grief!" Georgina practically screamed. "How could you just sit there on top of it?"

"I wasn't sure if I should tell." Walter glanced over his shoulder. "Some spirits don't like being told on, you know."

Georgina snatched the envelope out of his hands. It was addressed to Walter, care of his grandmother, Mrs. Fred Docker, and had come through the regular mail. The stamp was postmarked with the name of their town and the date of the day before. Inside, there was no letter, no note, no signature of any kind.

"Matches!" said Georgina, peering in. She shook three large wooden matches into her hand and examined them with critical eyes.

Poco stood up on tiptoes to see. "Oh, Walter," she said. "Do you think it's your mother?"

"I don't know."

"Spirits don't send messages to just anyone."

"Of course not." He glanced sideways at Georgina.

They had been walking along the sidewalk toward Poco's house. Now they came to a halt to decide what to do. Poco's mother had agreed to take them shopping at the mall. Not that they would be allowed to actually buy anything, but they could trail along behind her, looking at things. Mrs. Lambert was not so generous as their friend Angela Harrall's mother had been. Mrs. Harrall would have bought them magazines, and treated them to orange sodas as well. They missed her terribly—along with Angela, of course. Six months had passed since Angela had moved to Mexico, leaving her cat, Juliette, in Poco's care. It would be another six until she returned. "And she won't be the same," Poco had warned. "No one stays the same in far-off places like Mexico."

Now, as Poco held up one of the mysterious match sticks, a wave of excitement passed through the friends, and there was a sense of having found a far-off place nearer home.

"What do you think it means?" Walter asked. He tried to take the envelope back from Georgina, but she kept a grip on it.

"There's only one thing it can mean. The Match Girl wants to see you."

Walter nodded gravely. "That's what I thought."

"I'll go with you if you need me," Poco offered.

"I'll go whether you need me or not!" Georgina declared. "I think the Match Girl, whoever she is, meant this message for us all."

"She did?"

"Well, there are three matches, aren't there?"

This idea was questionable, but there was no time to argue. With her usual energy, Georgina leapt into action. She set off down the sidewalk at a rapid trot, barking back orders at her friends.

"First we'll go to Poco's house. We have to get out of going to the mall. Poco's mother won't like it, but that's too bad. We'll tell her we have more important things to do."

"George, wait! You can't tell her that!" Poco shrieked. Too late. She had already disappeared around the corner.

"Georgina is like one of those awful garden peacocks. Whenever anything happens, she spreads out and takes over," Poco complained as she and Walter raced along behind.

Luckily, they caught Georgina just before she rushed into the Lamberts' house. Poco managed to get inside first and talk to her mother. This was fortunate, because Mrs. Lambert was in a touchy mood and had to be coaxed, and promised, and apologized to. Finally she agreed, and Poco emerged from the house victorious, feeling as if she'd just handled a whole herd of peacocks.

It was a cool but sunny midafternoon when they arrived on foot at the park, and the sidewalks and lawns swarmed with people. The slides and swings were in heavy use. Two miniature sailboats skimmed across the pond. Some teenagers had set up a volleyball net and were playing a rousing game on the grass.

Thumbelina and the other bronze statues stood in the midst of all this activity, looking smugly as if they belonged. Only the Little Match Girl sat apart on her knoll at the park's far edge. Not a soul was near her, and perhaps even the park workers had forgotten she was there, because the grass around her was long and weedy with last year's growth. As they approached, the friends caught a wild smell of underbrush and overgrown bushes. It made them think of her lonely story.

"Didn't she freeze to death on New Year's Eve?" Georgina asked.

Poco nodded. "When she couldn't sell her matches, she huddled in an alley and began to light the matches herself to stay warm. She couldn't go home because her father would be angry."

"That's right. And each match she lit made a beautiful picture, and she could pretend she was inside it, warm and happy."

"Except she wasn't pretending. She was happy," Poco said. "Then her grandmother came and took her to heaven."

Walter, who had been listening with grave attention, suddenly cried out, "Look, what's that?"

They all saw it: the Little Match Girl statue had something in its ragged dress pocket, a white envelope like the one the matches had arrived in. Walter rushed forward and took it out.

"Let me see." Georgina made her usual grab. This time, Walter's hand flashed away behind his back.

"I will open it," he told her fiercely. "You may look, but I will do the opening." Poco saw that his elbow was trembling.

He brought the envelope out and turned it over. There was no writing on the front. At the back, the flap had been tucked in, not sealed. Walter untucked it and took something out. After he had gazed at it privately, he turned toward his friends and opened his hand. On his palm lay a tiny light blue mitten, knit in the smallest purls of yarn. A little blue button was sewn to the cuff. The mitten was smooth and clean, as if it had hardly ever been worn.

"I think it was knitted with toothpicks," Poco breathed.

"It's a baby's," Georgina said, and even she

sounded awed. "You button it onto the baby's snowsuit. Then the mitten can't fall off and get lost. Except"—she glanced up at Walter—"this one did fall off, I guess. Or Walter fell off and got lost from it, because . . ." She stopped.

Walter was having a struggle with his face. Under his baseball cap, his eyes kept opening wide, then narrowing down again. His mouth clamped into a line and quivered. This was strange behavior even for him, and the two friends looked away, embarrassed.

Then the struggle passed and Walter reached into his jeans pocket. For the hundredth time, he took out the photograph of his mother. Between the tips of his fingers he held it, fluttering a bit in the wind. He brought his other hand, the one holding the tiny mitten, up next to it. He stared at the photo, then at the mitten. Georgina and Poco came around and stared, too.

"I can't believe it," Georgina said, but there was no doubt. The light blue mitten looked exactly like the one the baby Walter was wearing in the photograph. They could even see the button attaching the mitten to the snowsuit.

"Who left this for you?" Georgina sounded outraged.

Poco glanced around the park. A feeling had come to her that they were being watched. The wind blew like a breath against her cheek. No one seemed to be near them, though. The volleyball game was in full sway. Some children were feeding a swan in the pond near the Ugly Duckling. Across the way, the Steadfast Tin Soldier had been surrounded by a noisy group of bicyclers entering at the gate. The sandwich shop was beyond, afternoon sunlight flashing in the windows.

Walter's hand had risen to his cheek. He had felt something, too. He didn't look frightened, though. He looked happy. He slipped the photo back into his pocket and, stepping closer to the Little Match Girl, touched her lightly on the shoulder.

"It's all right," he said. "I know who left the mitten."

"Who?" asked Georgina, glancing about with sharp eyes.

"My mother. She's here."

"Here?" Georgina jumped.

"Yes. I can feel her looking at me. She's watching to make sure I got her message." Walter gazed trustingly at the statue's bronze face. "My mother couldn't reach me on the regular ghost channel, so now she's decided to use the Little Match Girl instead."

FIVE

HOWEVER A PERSON chose to believe it was done, the arrival from the past of Walter's little blue mitten was a strange event. It went outside the normal lines of communication, even ghost communication, and made one wonder what unseen hand lay behind it.

"I don't like this!" Georgina wailed the next day after school. "This is not what I like to think about!"

"It's queer," Poco agreed. "And not only that. Someone was watching us. Walter was right."

"Could Walter's mother be rising up from her grave?"

"Where *is* her grave? We should find out."

Georgina shivered and curled against the couch. They were in Poco's living room, trying to do their homework. Schoolbooks lay on the floor at their feet, along with Juliette, Angela's big Siamese cat. Languorous snores rose from her sprawled furry body. Never had anyone seemed so sound asleep. But perhaps this was deceptive because, even as they looked, Juliette's powerful blue eyes cracked open. She lifted her head and stared at the friends.

"Stop that!" snapped Georgina, feeling an odd hypnotic tug.

"Watch out or she'll charm you," Poco warned. "Then she tries to control you with her thoughts. 'Go open a can of sardines and feed me.' 'Bring me a live mouse.' Suddenly, there you are hunting around in some field. It makes you worry what else she might have told you to do."

Georgina narrowed her eyes. "Oh, sure. Like what?"

"Well, anything. Why are you sitting here in my living room?"

"Because I wanted to come."

"Did you really decide that or did Juliette plant some message in your brain yesterday, when you were also here, if you remember. Maybe Juliette has a plan for us. Maybe, in a minute, we'll get up and carry it out."

"Maybe, in a minute, I'll get up and leave. Juliette can't stop me from doing that!"

"Unless she has already secretly commanded you to. Then you would just be carrying out her orders."

Georgina looked very upset at this but got up anyway and stamped into the hall. She went out the front door, slamming it so hard that no one could doubt that she was the one in charge— not some idiot Siamese feline.

Poco caught the cat's eye and smiled. Then she stood up and followed Georgina outside.

After weeks of shyly nosing around the edge, spring had finally decided to burst out into the open that day. The air smelled delicious. The sun blazed. Across the Lamberts' lawn, masses of tiny blue flowers waved their heads. In the midst of such forthright, open-air beauty, the very notion of ghosts seemed flimsy and unreal.

And yet there was Walter Kew, looking paler by the hour, receiving messages from a haunted statue in the park.

"He was there until dinner yesterday," Poco told Georgina after they had resettled on the porch. "And he went back this afternoon. He would spend the night there if he could."

"His grandmother has no idea what is happening. She loves Walter, but she's too old and deaf to notice. Walter is tuning out the real world. Have you seen his eyes?"

Poco nodded. "Pure white."

"Like a spirit's!" Georgina's voice fell to a whisper. "Do you think his dead mother is trying to take him away?"

This was such a cold and horrible thought that the friends sat frozen in silence for a moment. Then Poco spoke.

"We'll stay near him," Poco said. "We'll go where he goes and keep on talking whether he answers or not. That way he can't completely tune out. We'll be there reminding him he's on the planet Earth."

"All right." Georgina gave a purposeful sniff. "We should also try to find out some facts. I mean about his real mother, who used to be alive. Who was she and why doesn't anyone know?"

"There is someone we could ask—old Miss Bone."

"Miss Bone!" Georgina cried. "I forgot about her."

She was the retired schoolteacher who was living at Angela Harrall's house while the family was away.

"She seemed to know something when we saw her last winter," Poco said. "Remember how she said, 'So, you are Walter Kew!' as if something had happened long ago. Walter was always too scared to ask any more about it."

"Let's go and see her this afternoon. She's halfway to the park anyway. Afterward we can go and find Walter."

They went to tell Poco's mother their plans, then started off. But they were hardly out the door when Mrs. Lambert called them back and insisted that Juliette go with them on her leash.

"Juliette! But how . . ." Georgina spun around. She caught sight of the cat spying on them from the living room. The old fleabag was watching their every move.

"But we can't take her!" Poco protested. "Juliette never wants to walk in a straight line."

Mrs. Lambert's mind was made up, though. Or had been made up for her, Georgina thought grimly.

"Miss Bone has been asking for Juliette," Mrs. Lambert said. "She took a special interest in her after the poor thing was lost for all those months in the cold. This is the perfect time to bring her by."

"Oh, all right!" Poco stamped into the living room.

Juliette looked at them smugly as they hooked on her leash. The cat had aged since her odd disappearance and even stranger return last winter. Her fur wasn't so neat and well-groomed. She slept a lot more and stayed closer to home. Now, however, some new mood had struck. Outside, on the sidewalk, she padded along with bright eyes, never once veering off course. This made Georgina so nervous that she slowed down and walked several steps behind.

"Is Juliette still wearing that weird charm that was on her when she came back from being lost?" she asked.

"Right here on her collar." Poco smoothed away the fur under the cat's chin to reveal a little silver box. "Angela didn't believe me when I told her, but I know invisible beings put it there. Juliette is a cat in touch with the unknown." She noted with pleasure that Georgina had dropped back a little farther.

"How is Angela anyway?" Georgina shouted up. "She never calls me anymore."

"She was sick with a terrible stomachache. For months and months she couldn't eat anything. But now she's better, except her voice sounds different. Thinner, sort of."

"Hmm."

"George, why are you walking back there?" Poco asked in a voice that was not entirely sincere. "Are you scared of something? I can hardly hear you."

There was no answer at all to this question. Poco pressed her lips together with satisfaction and strode ahead energetically.

It was not easy to be going back to Angela's house after all the trouble there last winter. When the friends knocked on Miss Bone's garage apartment door, their hearts began to race.

Luckily, she did not make them wait. Poco's careful mother had phoned ahead, and the old woman opened the door immediately.

"Hello. Hello. How sweet of you to come!"

She was wearing a turban on her head, and a long black skirt with old-fashioned lace-up shoes. This was the sort of outfit that once would have convinced the friends of dark plots and evil intent. Now:

"Hello, Miss Bone. You look great! Just like yourself."

"Why, thank you! I'm so pleased to see you both. And Juliette! You old sorceress. Have you recovered from your vanishing act?"

"Yes she has. A little too well, we are beginning to think. She's back to her old mysterious ways," Poco said. She saw how Miss Bone's knobby hand went directly to the cat's neck and felt around in the thick fur.

Georgina saw it, too. "I guess you heard about the charm Juliette had on when she came home," she told Miss Bone pointedly. "It has catnip inside. A sign of invisibles. Poco believes they are keeping Juliette safe."

"Invisibles, did you say? As in fairies and elves?" Miss Bone smiled. "Well, why not? I'm sure it's so."

"I'm not," Georgina said as they walked upstairs. "I think someone in the real world put the charm on her."

"Good heavens, why do a thing like that?" Miss Bone held open the door. "You are far too suspicious, Georgina. Always on the trail of something. Or someone," she added sharply, causing both girls to blush. "But where is your third investigator, that nice boy Walter Kew?"

"It's about Walter that we've come," Poco said. "He's having a problem with his mother. We wondered if you knew something about her."

"His mother!" Miss Bone turned abruptly on her heel. "Has she come back, then, after all these years?"

"Well, yes," Poco said. "In a way, she has."

SIX

"OF COURSE I know nothing. Nothing that Walter hasn't heard a hundred times, I'm sure," Miss Bone said, settling into a kitchen chair. She reached down and picked up Juliette, who was pleased and immediately curled up in her lap.

"But that's the trouble. He hasn't heard anything," Georgina said. "His grandmother has never told him one fact about his parents. There are no photos either, nothing passed down or left behind. Walter doesn't have the slightest clue where he comes from."

"It's made him a little crazy, if you want to know," Poco added.

"I can understand," Miss Bone said. "I'd feel unsettled myself if I'd arrived that way on a doorstep. And in a casserole dish! Now there's a recipe for mystery."

"A casserole dish!" Poco and Georgina cried together.

"Hasn't Walter ever told you? I'm sorry I spoke. Perhaps he's sensitive about it."

"No he's not! He doesn't know," Georgina exclaimed.

"Doesn't know! That's impossible. It's not the kind of thing you can keep from a child."

But apparently it was. Granny Docker had never breathed a word, as Walter himself was soon explaining. While Juliette stayed and was petted by Miss Bone, Poco and Georgina ran to the park and found him. He was hovering as usual by the Little Match Girl.

"Come, quick! Miss Bone's told us something about you."

"Miss Bone?"

"She knows how you came to your grandmother's house."

He was suspicious and went unwillingly at first. But half an hour later, with everyone gathered in Miss Bone's little kitchen, he gazed in astonishment at the elderly woman.

"A casserole dish! But how could I fit in?" he asked, as if there weren't a hundred more important questions.

"Oh, well, it was a large one," Miss Bone replied. "Your grandmother was famous for it. Whenever a big dinner was given in town, she was asked to cook something in that dish. I remember that her Macaroni and Cheese took two women to carry. Her Chicken Tetrazzini needed three."

Carried by three women! Walter trembled at the thought. He had set his sights so firmly on one. "But how . . . but where . . . my mother . . . when?"

"Of course the casserole had been emptied, and the dish washed and dried, by the time you got into it," Miss Bone assured him. "I forget what it was we had for dinner that night. Noodles Romanov, maybe. Or Tuna Supreme?" She tapped her finger thoughtfully on the table.

"It was a plain old church supper, you see. Your

grandmother went home early without the dish, leaving it to the washup crew. Which happened that night to be only me." Miss Bone gave an embarrassed laugh. "I hardly knew old Mrs. Docker—and still don't, I'm afraid—but when she came to me the next day to ask if I had seen . . ."

Miss Bone stopped and shook her head. "You must go to her yourself," she said to Walter. "It's not my place to be telling such things."

"Oh yes! Please!" Walter grasped her arm. "My grandmother won't tell me anything. I think she's forgotten. If you could just say how I got in the dish . . ."

"Well, that's the whole problem, isn't it?"

"What do you mean?" Walter's eyes were wide as saucers.

"I mean no one knows. Or at least I don't. It's a puzzle to this very day. I left the dish in the church pantry, clean as a whistle. The next morning, there it was at your granny's front door, filled to the brim with little pink you. Until now, I never told anyone. It was a touchy subject, and not my affair."

THEY HAD to carry Juliette home. Something came over her at Miss Bone's apartment, and when they got up to leave, she would not walk. She just sat and blinked at Walter in a dazed sort of way, no matter how they yanked on her leash.

"It was hearing about the casserole being carried by three women," gasped Georgina, staggering along the sidewalk under the cat's weight. "Juliette suddenly realized there was a better way to travel." Angela's pet was twice as large as an ordinary Siamese. Like Angela herself, she had always gone in for extra helpings at mealtimes.

"Please don't make jokes when Juliette can hear," Poco said severely. She was walking alongside, holding on to the leash, which was still attached to Juliette's collar, for some reason. "The trip to Miss Bone's was too far for her, that's all. She's not as young as she used to be."

They turned around to look for Walter, who was lagging behind in a daze himself.

"He's just begun to figure out that if Miss Bone's story is true, his grandmother is not his real grandmother," Poco whispered to Georgina.

"Good grief. That's right!"

"Next he'll see that his grandfather was not his real grandfather."

Georgina took this opportunity to hand Juliette to Poco, who was so short that the cat's tail hung below her knees as they walked along. For a few minutes neither one of them could talk— Georgina because she was recovering her strength, and Poco because she was about to fall over. Finally, Georgina got her wind back.

"There is something else—Walter's parents' terrible accident. If Granny Docker never knew who left Walter at the door, how could she know how his parents died?"

"She couldn't. Maybe they just got sick."

"Or hanged themselves or jumped off a cliff." Georgina tended to think in more drastic terms. "No one would want to tell a little child that. Or maybe they never were killed at all."

Poco was shocked. "What do you mean?"

"Well, I guess they might still be somewhere alive."

This was such a startling thought that Poco's grip loosened. Suddenly Juliette was slipping through her arms. With a terrific thud, the cat landed. And lay still.

"Oh no! Juliette! I'm so sorry!"

"Is she dead?" Georgina asked, leaning over hopefully.

Walter came up then. Without a word, he gathered Juliette into his arms. He carried her the rest of the way, far more easily—and more comfortably, no doubt—than either of the girls. Walter was thin, but his arms were strong. By the time they arrived at Poco's house, the cat was smiling and cuddling up to him, as if this was where she'd wanted to be from the beginning.

Georgina looked on in disgust. "I think Juliette is a cat who gets what she wants."

"Oh, she is," Poco agreed. "She always has been."

Walter nodded. "Juliette has powers we can't even imagine."

"She told me once that she expects to live hundreds of lives," Poco said. "Not just the miserable nine usually handed out to cats. She even asked if I'd consider coming along."

"Along where?" Georgina said in alarm.

"To the next life. Wasn't that sweet? I told her I'd have to think about it. I wouldn't want to leave now, anyway, not when I'm just in the middle of this one."

"You wouldn't?" asked Georgina, with a look of relief.

"Oh no. But how nice of you to worry. I wouldn't have thought you really cared."

"Who says I do?" Georgina humphed, but without much force. She'd had a sudden vision of Poco vanishing through the walls into dazzling, invisible, unknown worlds—while she was left stranded on the dull, earthly side. Perhaps Georgina had grown more used to Poco than she knew, because the idea of being without her, even for a day, seemed all at once very upsetting.

"Will you teach me how to talk to Juliette?" she found herself asking a minute later.

Poco's mouth all but dropped open. "Georgina!" she cried in a sort of horror. It was so completely unlike her friend. "When do you think you'd want to start?"

"Oh, no hurry." Georgina seemed suddenly to have second thoughts. She even began to look embarrassed. "I'd just sometime like to hear what thoughts go on inside a pelt."

"A pelt! Wait a minute. That is not very nice. . . ."

They passed the rest of the walk in a more comfortable state of battle.

WALTER KEW had no sooner heard Miss Bone's story about the casserole dish than he knew what he had to do. He had to find it. He had to touch it and lift it and look inside, and generally make sure that it truly did exist.

"But why?" Georgina could not understand. And she was tired. They had all just come into Poco's house after the long walk from Miss Bone's apartment. "By now it's probably a cracked, greasy old thing."

"I don't care," Walter said. "I have to see where I was." He looked down at Juliette, who lay like a great furry baby in his arms. "And you and Poco have to see, too."

Georgina groaned. "Can't we look the next time we're there?"

Walter shook his head. They must see it right now. Only someone delivered to a strange house in the middle of the night could appreciate why.

"Your grandmother's house isn't strange. It's the only place you've ever lived!" Georgina sat down in Poco's living room.

"It was strange when Walter was first left on the porch," Poco said. "Imagine how he must have felt lying there and waiting in the casserole dish. I hope they didn't put the lid on."

Georgina yawned. "I don't believe he felt anything. He was much too little to know what was happening."

"Oh no I wasn't!" Walter's pale eyes flashed. "I might not have been able to talk yet, but I felt things. I worried about why I was outside in the cold instead of in my usual warm bed. I worried about where my mother had gone. I worried about when she was coming back and what was going to happen to me next. Babies get worried and frightened, you know, even if later they can't exactly remember."

Several minutes passed before Georgina could get this idea into her head. Babies had always seemed like pink lumps to her. Cute, yes, but completely stupid. "As long as they're fed and have their diapers changed—"

She was drowned out by protests from Poco and Walter. Even Juliette turned to glare at her.

"All right. I'll go!" Georgina hastily stood up.

And so, not long after the friends had arrived, they set out again, this time for Walter's house. Walter was in such a state of impatience that he galloped ahead on the sidewalk. He took off his baseball cap and ran fearless under the sun, a thing Georgina and Poco had never seen him do. They followed at a distance, wondering at the power of one casserole dish to so change the behavior of their shy and shadowy friend.

SEVEN

MRS. DOCKER was such a dear, frail, gentle old granny that it was impossible to enter her house in any way other than on tiptoes. She was quite deaf, and the silence in her head had gradually, over the years, spilled out to make a silence all around her—a silence in which the hall clock ticked, and mice scrambled in the walls, and everyone spoke in whispers—unless you spoke to Granny, that is. Then you shouted at the top of your lungs. This is what Walter did as soon as he found his grandmother in the kitchen, her deep-lined face bent close over an ironing board.

"Granny!"

"Oh!"

"It's me, Walter!"

"Oh, Walter! You scared me. I was just ironing your shirts."

"This is Georgina!"

"Who?"

"And Poco!"

"What?"

"My friends. You've met them before, remember?"

Granny peered cautiously around Walter. Suddenly her face brightened.

"Oh, Georgina. And Poco. How nice to see you. I was just ironing Walter's shirts."

They shook hands pleasantly. Mrs. Docker was an old-fashioned sort of granny who liked that sort of thing. She had wonderful manners, though, and was soon offering them lemonade and a jar full of homemade cookies. Then she went back to her ironing board, and for a few minutes the silence poured out of her again, and every creak and chew could be heard in the kitchen. Georgina and Poco looked nervously at Walter.

"Granny!" he shouted at last. They all jumped. More softly, but urgently, he said, "Granny, I want to see the big casserole dish."

Something new in the tone of his voice must have come through to her, because the old woman set the iron down and stared at him. All at once, from beneath her oldness and wrinkles, a younger woman seemed to look out with anxious eyes.

"What do you want it for?" she asked. "It's been stored away since your grandfather died."

"Just to look."

Granny gazed at him for a second more, then nodded. "Well, why not?" she muttered, more to herself than to him. "I'd like a look myself after all this time. It's in the pantry," she said, turning to Georgina, "pushed back a good way under the counter."

The casserole was there, all right. From a distant corner came a glint, as if a large, mysterious animal had blinked in the dark. It was far too heavy for one person to pick up, or even to drag out into daylight. The efforts of all three children were necessary to hold the low pantry door open and to yank and pull the old cooking dish through. Poco lifted the huge ceramic cover off while the others hoisted the bottom part onto the kitchen table. Then she lowered the top back on and—there it stood.

"My casserole dish," Walter announced proudly. "Not cracked or greasy at all. Just a little dusty."

Creepy, Georgina might have said, but she kept quiet.

Walter brought a sponge from the sink and wiped the dish down a bit. The sides were a deep blue with wavy white lines painted around them. The cover matched, except that its lines were spokes that fanned out from the center knob. Walter lifted the top again and gazed inside for a long moment; then he turned to his grandmother, who seemed rooted in place.

"Who brought me, Granny?" he asked her in the quiet new tone that somehow she heard so well. "You'll tell me, won't you? I need to know."

Perhaps it was having all of them there staring at her. Perhaps it was simply the casserole dish, sitting big and bold in her kitchen again after all the years gone by. Whatever did it, Granny Docker heard Walter so clearly that her hands flew up to cover her ears, as if they'd been pierced by the words he said. Then, slowly, she took her hands away.

"I made Chicken Wiggle that night," she began, and it was a good thing the friends had been to see Miss Bone or they might have laughed and spoiled everything. Chicken Wiggle was not a dish anyone had heard of before.

"It's a fine old recipe—boiled chicken, cream sauce, peas, and so on," Granny said, "and I'd worked all afternoon cooking and boning. I was tired when we went to the church in the evening. Walter's grandfather carried the casserole in. Single-handed, he did it! I remember so well."

A fond look crept over her face, then changed to sadness. They all saw how she missed her husband. For a moment her silence threatened to pour out again, but Granny caught herself and pushed it back down.

"An ordinary church supper it was, nothing special," she went on. "Or so we thought as we sat and ate. Later your grandfather and I went over everything, who was there that night, who might have known, who had the chance to make such a delivery. We were never able to come up with one clue."

"What delivery?" Walter cut in. "Please tell what happened."

"We went home early," Granny answered. "Miss Emma Bone was to do the washing up. Next morning I was to go by the church and collect the empty dish. We'd arranged it all, but during the night . . ."

Granny paused and looked at Walter.

"During the night..," she began again, and got no further.

"During the night," she said a third time, her voice beginning to tremble. "During the night . . . well, during the night, magic happened!"

"Magic?"

"You!" whispered Granny, touching him suddenly on his cheek. "You were there on the porch when I opened the door next morning, tucked down into this very dish. 'Heavens!' I cried, and nearly jumped out of my skin. Your grandfather rushed out. Then we saw the folded note. We burned it later, but I'll never forget what it said:

For safety's sake, tell no one how I came.
Guard me and keep me. Walter is my name."

Under his baseball cap, Walter had turned pale. If his friends had recently worried about the ghost world taking him over, now they were afraid of what the real world might do.

"Walter, don't feel bad. We'll be your friends, no matter who you are," Poco said in his ear.

"After all, you could be a millionaire!" Georgina exclaimed. "Or a prince or the son of a famous person."

Walter stared at Granny. "So you are not my real grandmother?" he asked, as if he had only now come to fully believe it.

She shook her head sadly.

"And you don't know who my real mother was?"

"No."

"And my grandfather was never my real grandfather?"

"I'm so sorry."

"And my parents were never killed in a terrible accident. You said that to keep me from knowing the truth," Walter said, his voice rising.

"Well, yes, but . . ."

"And you never told me anything," Walter began to shout. "Even when I asked. Even though it was my own special, one-of-a-kind life and you had no right to hide it from me all this time!"

Granny looked stricken. "I didn't think of it that way," she quavered. "You were so small. You needed protection. "'Guard me,' the note said. 'For safety's sake.' We didn't dare say a word. We pretended you were our grandson. No one ever came forward to claim you. We'd never been able to have a baby of our own. You came from the church like an answer from . . ."

But Walter could no longer listen to her reasons. He was angry, angrier than Georgina and Poco had ever seen him. The kitchen suddenly grew too tight to hold him. Like a small, furious rocket, he blasted into the living room, where he ran in two maddened circles around the couch. Then he exploded with a great cry of rage and ran out the front door into the yard. They heard his footsteps slam against the walk and fade down the street.

When he had gone, Granny sighed and went again into the quiet of her head. Her eyes became the old foggy ones they all knew, and her ears went as dead as if they were stuffed with cotton. She turned back to the ironing board and picked up her iron, and silence rose like thick, gray dust through the kitchen.

"Good-bye, Mrs. Docker," Georgina murmured politely.

"Thank you for the cookies," Poco said.

Granny did not look up, so they tiptoed through the house and let themselves softly out the front door.

EIGHT

WALTER DID NOT COME to
school the next day. He did not come the day
after that either, which was a rainy Friday.
Spring showers had arrived. All morning it
poured, and then all afternoon.

After lunch, classes were sent to watch a
nature movie in the gym. This was wonderful
for Poco, who had always wanted to know about
the feeding habits of the Patagonian mole rat,
but a misery for Georgina. She scratched and
jiggled and twisted in her seat, and was finally

sent to the hall for kicking the person in front of her.

"I'm so worried about Walter," she whispered to Poco when their classes filed by in opposite directions. "What should we do?"

"Wait," Poco whispered back. "He needs time to think."

So they waited—all Friday afternoon at Poco's house while the rain thundered down; all Saturday night at Georgina's, where Poco slept over and a drizzle continued. By Sunday morning, which dawned clear, there had still been no word. The friends walked by Walter's house after breakfast. He wasn't sitting on his porch or hanging around his yard.

"Should we knock?" Georgina asked.

"Well, all right. Let me do it." Poco went to the door and gave a timid rap. There was no answer.

"Knock louder," Georgina insisted. "Maybe Granny will hear."

Poco rapped a bit harder. "I don't think anyone's home. Maybe Walter's gone to the park."

"The park!" Georgina shivered. "Do we have to go there?"

"We should go," Poco said. "We're his only friends."

They walked over after lunch, taking the streets they knew he would choose, in case he was already walking back. They reached the park gates without seeing him, and a minute later their hopes were dashed. On her knoll the Little Match Girl huddled alone. They walked across to her anyway. Her dress pockets were filled with rainwater. Grass and weeds had grown over her knees. Poco cleared away a vine that had begun to climb up one arm.

"Why don't the park workers look after her the way they do the other statues?" she asked. "She is twice as beautiful, even if she is sad."

"She's too far away," Georgina replied. "And the hill is too steep. The workers can't get their mowers up here. She was put in the wrong place—that's why she's left out."

This seemed to Poco so very unfair that she threaded her arm through the statue's, if only to give the lonely figure some kindness. And there, as her hand brushed against the Match Girl's cool, bronze hand, she felt something move. She leaned forward and saw a ring on one of the molded fingers.

"Georgina, look!"

It was made not of bronze but of some brighter

: **65**

metal, though covered with a film of grime. If Poco had not touched it, she would never have known it was there.

"It's old," she said. "Look at this design. It reminds me of my mother's high school ring." She tried to pull it off, but the ring would not pass over the first molded knuckle.

"Maybe it was always there," Georgina said, after she had looked closely. "Maybe the sculptor put it on when he made the statue."

"I don't think so. It's a real gold ring. See how it shines when I clean off the dirt? Gold is the only metal that never tarnishes."

They took turns polishing, using the edges of their shirts. Finally, the gold blazed with its warm, true color. The Match Girl's face seemed to light up, too, as if she were bending over one of her own matches.

Poco sat back. "Do you ever get the feeling that there's someone . . . well . . ."

"Inside?" Georgina gazed at the statue's pretty face. She hadn't thought of it before, but, "The Match Girl looks about the same age as we are."

"Yes! And now she wants to come out and talk."

"But she's afraid because she's sat on this hill

for so long and been kept apart from all the other statues."

Poco nodded. "That's why she showed us her ring. She hopes we'll come to visit her again."

"Oh, we will!" cried Georgina, addressing the bronze girl. "We promise we won't let you be alone. You can tell us what really happened in your story. I never did understand why you sat there and froze."

This was such an enchanting fantasy that the friends kept on with it for nearly an hour, even making up answers the Little Match Girl might give. And though outwardly she never revealed a thing, they began to feel they were getting to know her. Georgina sighed and looked around.

"Where *is* Walter? I was sure he'd come if we waited."

"Let's start walking back. Maybe we'll see him."

On the way out of the park, they had a sudden thought and crossed the street to the sandwich shop. The nice waitress was behind the counter.

"Yes? Can I help?" She stepped forward as they entered.

"We are looking for our friend," Poco explained. "The boy who was with us before.

He comes here sometimes to buy candy and we wondered . . ."

"No, he hasn't come." The waitress moved closer. "Not for four days. Is something wrong?"

"We're not sure."

"He was coming every day. Not here, of course." She waved a hand around the store. "To the park. I saw him every afternoon, going in, coming out. He went to the statue or sat by the pond."

"You could see him from here?" Georgina said in surprise. "I can hardly even see the Little Match Girl."

Everyone turned and stared out the window. Streams of people were going in at the gate. Inside, the pathways were filling up with Sunday walkers. If Walter came now, they could never pick him out, one small boy lost in the shuffle.

"I'm sure he's all right," Poco told the waitress. "The park is a little way from his house. He probably didn't want to walk in the rain." She wasn't going to say what had really happened.

"Oh yes. The rain. But today is nice."

The swinging doors to the sandwich shop's back room flew apart. The old man came through and took up his post behind the meat case. He gave the waitress such a threatening look that she moved away and began to wipe the counter. The friends made for the front door. They left without daring even to say good-bye.

"I feel so sorry for that poor waitress," Georgina said on the way home.

"That man is the meanest-looking person," Poco agreed. "I guess he must be the owner of the shop."

"Did you see how she jumped when he came in? She's scared of him. I would quit that job and go work somewhere else."

Poco didn't answer. She was gazing at something in the distance.

"Look!" she cried. "Here he comes!"

"Where!" shouted Georgina, who thought she meant Walter.

"My robin!" Poco cried. "The one who spent the winter here. He just flew into that maple tree. Hello! Hello! I'm so glad to see you! I was beginning to think you hadn't made it through!" She ran toward the tree.

Georgina looked up and saw not one robin but a large flock coming in for a landing. There must have been twenty red-breasted birds fluttering, changing branches, chirping furiously at one another. No one could possibly have told them apart.

Or could they? As Georgina watched, Poco stopped under the tree. A robin hopped to a low branch and gave out a piercing squawk that made her laugh. Then began one of the loudest, friendliest, and most embarrassing bird conversations that Georgina had ever heard, and she had suffered through quite a few in her time with Poco.

"See you later," she shouted over the racket. "You know I can't stand this."

"I know," Poco yelled back. "Isn't he great, though? He knows the funniest jokes."

"How could you tell it was him?" Georgina couldn't help asking. "He looks exactly like all the others to me."

"It's easy," Poco said, smiling up at the bird. "Once you get to love a robin, you can spot him anywhere."

NINE

POCO LAMBERT was a good person, and sometimes amazingly wise, but she was not always reliable. When she got onto bird talk, or happened to run into one of the five hundred rabbits she knew around town, she could forget about everything else in the world. At such times there had to be someone to step in—someone smart, sensible, and willing to work alone. (Georgina thought this masterfully to herself as she continued along the sidewalk.)

There had to be someone who was never distracted or afraid to take risks. (Georgina walked straight to Walter's house and marched up the front path.) Someone to pound on doors (Georgina pounded on Walter's door) and to coax stubborn people out of hiding for their own good.

"Walter Kew! I know you're in there," Georgina bellowed on the front porch. "Open up or I'll start screaming!"

A muffled noise came from deep inside. Moments later the door drifted open and a white hand floated into the breach. It was followed by the pale figure of . . . a ghost! Georgina jumped and let out a shriek.

"Georgina! Good grief!" The ghost covered its ears.

"Walter? Is that you? Wait, don't close the door." She recovered in time to force her foot over the threshold. A brief struggle broke out. Walter's face appeared from under his cap. He looked terrible, tired and rumpled, and so thin there seemed hardly anything left of him. Georgina was shocked. She grew more upset as the visit wore on. For despite his ghastly, ghostly appearance, Walter was no longer in touch with his invisible worlds.

72 :

"He's stopped believing in spirits," Georgina told Poco in hollow tones on the telephone that evening. "And he's quitting school. Everyone hates him, he says."

"That's crazy. Where is Granny Docker?"

"She's come out of her fog and is trying to talk to him. I think she's really worried, but he won't listen."

"Did you tell him about the Match Girl's ring?"

"Yes. He doesn't care. He says he'll never go there again. The mitten, the matches, everything was a lie."

"A lie! What does he mean?"

"He said his ghost-mother was someone his own mind invented. The same with his spirits— he made them up. And the Match Girl's message was a trick someone played. It could be Miss Bone or Granny—or us! He doesn't trust anyone anymore. The baby mitten is too new to be his, he says. And the photo was never really of him. Granny told him that to cover up the real truth."

Poco's heart sank. "What is the real truth?"

"That he wasn't good enough." Georgina took a deep breath. "Walter thinks he wasn't good enough to be somebody's child, and that's why his parents gave him away. Oh, Poco, it's just what you said—he's lost all his stories. And now he's too sad to invent any more, so I guess he'll just slowly shrivel up and, you know . . . like the little rabbits." Her voice trailed off. They sat in silence.

"Are you missing Juliette, by any chance?" Georgina remembered to ask after a while. "I thought I saw her running along the sidewalk when I was going to Walter's. She looked as if she was heading for the park."

"It couldn't have been Juliette," Poco said. "Juliette doesn't run anywhere anymore. She just keeps getting older and slower. My mother is worried she won't make it until Angela comes back from Mexico."

This struck such a final dreary note that the friends shortly decided to hang up. Outside, spring rain had begun to fall again. All over town, homeowners closed their windows and braced for the new downpour. People passing on the sidewalks raised their umbrellas and lowered their eyes to avoid stepping in puddles. It was for this reason that no one saw the strange gray shadow that shot up the path to Walter's house and paused by the mail basket next to the door. The rain came down harder. The shadow whisked away.

TEN

AT FIRST, Walter Kew really did seem to have quit school. For a week he was absent without explanation. When, finally, he did come back ("Because otherwise he'd be arrested," as Georgina said), he kept himself so invisible that even Poco had trouble finding him. He was a shape in the corner, a blur on the stairs, an anonymous figure at the back of a room. And if, by chance, someone did catch up with him, it was only a matter of time before he slipped away. Houdini himself might have wondered how it was done.

None of this was especially new. For years Walter had been a master of invisibility, as people often are who have long been ignored. Rather than be snubbed, they learn to step aside or, better yet, to make it appear they have never been there at all. Now Walter seemed to have perfected the art. He would not be seen and—

"He will not talk!" Georgina raged in exasperation. "No matter what I say. Walter hears but he looks away—as if I'm the one that's turning invisible!"

"That would be impossible," Poco assured her.

They were walking along the sidewalk toward the park. For some reason, without Walter, they found themselves going there more often. After the fussy crafts of Girl Scouts or a polite piano lesson, they would go together in the late afternoon. The Little Match Girl had a sharper, realer air around her. It wasn't only her story— "Remember, she dies," Poco said—but a sense that there really was someone still there, caught inside, crying out for attention if only they could understand her. But whether this was connected to the Little Match Girl's trouble, or to some more recent sadness, they could not tell.

They couldn't go every day. Their schedules

were so busy. Four days or a week might pass. But then:

"The Little Match Girl needs weeding," Poco would announce. Or:

"I saw a ring in a store that looked a little like . . ." Georgina did not even need to finish. Off they went to the knoll, though it felt odd to be always visiting without Walter. And once, in the distance, they were sure they saw him—until the person turned and walked the other way.

"I guess he really has given her up." Georgina sighed.

"But someone else hasn't." Poco glanced over her shoulder.

They felt themselves being watched every time they came. There was no telling how or from where. Or by whom.

"Is it our imaginations?" Georgina whispered. She glanced protectively at the Little Match Girl.

Poco shook her head. "People always know when they're being spied on. Animals do, too. Try staring at a rabbit when he isn't looking. In a little while he'll turn around and find you."

"What is it?" Georgina asked. "An invisible ray?"

"No one knows," Poco answered. "But this watcher is real."

Under normal circumstances, this would have been enough to scare Georgina away. She did not like what could not be explained. A closely watched statue holding strange secrets was not the sort of company she cared to keep. But in this case, now that Walter no longer cared:

"The Match Girl needs us." That was all she could say.

Besides, the knoll had become their special territory. There was something to be said for lonely, out-of-the-way places, for standing apart and simply observing. The statue's little rise put the whole park at their feet. They saw who came and where they went. People often did things you wouldn't expect—they shouted, then kissed, or laughed and wept; they petted their dogs, then turned around and hit them. A serious man came in a gray business suit. He set his briefcase on the grass and took off his jacket. Then with the spring of a circus performer, he kicked up his heels and stood on his head. For nearly a minute, he balanced that way, grinning upside down at the people who passed him. At last, he righted himself and put his jacket back on, smoothed his hair, picked up his briefcase, and returned as he had come.

78 :

Georgina and Poco gazed after him in amazement.

And then there was the work the girls found themselves doing, because fascinating though it was, who could just sit forever looking? Without meaning to, they became the Match Girl's gardeners.

The dead grass around her knees was their first project. It was so yellow, so ragged. They yanked it out. But this only made the other weeds look worse. They tackled huge clumps with their bare hands. Later, wielding a pair of Mrs. Lambert's clippers, they cut back the bushes engulfing the statue's head. ("Oh!" cried Georgina. "She looks so much better!") They even managed to snip out a sort of lawn. It spread like a carpet from the Match Girl's skirt; just a small square of green, but it gave her respectability.

By the time this was finished, June had come. With flowers blooming all over town, the friends began to think of planting their own.

"Wildflowers," Poco said, as they walked up the knoll that day. "Not the delicate ones that people put in gardens."

"Yes, she would like the kind that have to live by themselves," Georgina replied.

They set about clearing another overgrown patch of ground. But the earth had hardened after a week of bright sun, and they could no longer work it with their hands.

"Tomorrow, we'll bring shovels," Poco said. "Did you notice those daisies along the road? We could dig some up and plant them here."

"We have poppies in our backyard," Georgina offered. "My mother hates them and wouldn't care what we took." They both turned and glanced at the Match Girl's face. Perhaps it was the light, but somehow she looked pleased.

And so the project went forward. As the days passed, an assortment of wildflowers from various back lots began to appear around the crest of the knoll. Their wispy clumps shriveled and all but died the first week, until the gardeners learned the importance of water. Even wild things, it seemed, required looking after.

The friends took turns lugging a plastic bucket up from the pond, ignoring the curious looks of the miniature-boat people. Once they were intercepted by a park security guard, but it was too hot that day to worry about the theft of a few pails of water. Mopping his brow, he let them go. For the most part, they tended the knoll unnoticed. And the Match Girl kept her silence, revealing nothing more.

School entered its final, sluggish crawl before the summer vacation. Georgina and Poco had begun to wonder if Walter Kew would ever speak to them again, when, without warning, he slid up beside Poco one afternoon as she walked home alone from school. Georgina was attending a last Girl Scout meeting.

"Walter!" It had been so long. The air around him had an unfamiliar flutter. "Is everything all right?"

"Yes."

They walked half a block before Poco dared to ask if there was something—well, something he wanted to tell her?

"Yes."

"Well, what?" (By now, Georgina would be yelling.)

"Can you come to my house? Everything is there."

"Everything?" Poco felt a surge of excitement. "But Georgina . . ."

: 81

"I know." Walter's pale eyes rested on her face. "If you don't mind, could you come by yourself?"

In a great rush, Poco felt how much she liked him. She had almost forgotten his fine politeness. As they trudged along the sidewalk toward the Dockers' house, the old comfort of their friendship began to come back.

"Are you speaking to Granny again?" she asked when they entered the silent, clock-ticking house.

Walter shrugged. "She bought a hearing aid. She said she wanted to hear me better." They put their heads through the kitchen door and saw her bustling over the stove.

"Come on," Walter whispered, pulling Poco away. "You know the photo of me and my mother? Granny said it came with me in the big casserole. She said she's sorry she waited to show me. I had a right to know who I was."

Poco nodded.

"She also told me how I got my last name. My grandfather gave it to me."

"I always wondered why it wasn't Docker."

"My grandfather used to call me Walter Q., short for Questionmark, because I was such a mystery. Then other people began to call me that, too, even though no one knew what it meant. In the end, my grandfather decided I should have it for my own. So he spelled it out: K-E-W."

Poco smiled. "That's a great story."

"I know," Walter said. "And there's a lot more."

They ran upstairs to his room. He opened the door with a nervous flourish.

"My collection," he announced.

He might just as well have said, "My crown jewels." They were laid on his bed like priceless diamonds: the huge casserole dish and the tiny mitten. The photo in the park and . . .

"Walter, what are these?"

"The Little Match Girl is giving me presents again. One by one, she's giving me back my things."

"The Match Girl! But how? You've been going to the park?"

"Yes, whenever I get a message."

"What message?"

"Wooden matches. The same as before."

"But how . . . ?"

"I've seen you and Georgina there. I went away

whenever you came. Don't worry, I like all the work you've done. The Match Girl looks better. And I saw the ring."

"Walter! Why did you never tell us?"

He kept his eyes down and wouldn't answer.

"Is it your mother?" Poco whispered. "Is she back again?"

"Yes, she's here!" He looked up to see if she would believe him.

Poco knelt to inspect the items. There was a locket shaped like a tiny book that opened on silver hinges. Inside were two miniature photographs. One was of a baby with fat cheeks. In the other, a man was wearing a soldier's uniform. Walter watched over her shoulder.

"I think it's me again, and maybe . . ."

"Your father?"

"I'm not sure," Walter said carefully.

There was a pair of fuzzy socks with blue satin bows, and a matching sweater small enough for a doll.

"Don't tell anyone," Walter begged. "I know this stuff is stupid. Don't tell Georgina. She'd laugh if she saw it."

"She might not," Poco said.

"But she might."

84 :

There was a cheap plastic rattle with a clown's head at one end, the kind that came out of the discount bins. Walter watched anxiously when Poco lifted it up.

"Incredible," she whispered, and gently replaced it.

Finally, there was a baby's hospital bracelet made of blue and white beads. "W-A-L-T-E-R," the white beads spelled.

"I have one of these." It was so little that Poco could hold it on her palm. "But mine has pink beads and my last name is on it, Lambert."

"What's it for?"

"The hospital nurses put it on you when you're born. There are always a lot of babies in the hospital. The nurses want to make sure your right mother takes you home."

This comment had a strange effect on Walter. He began to walk around the room, swinging his arms like a powerful windmill. For a moment Poco had a vision of the sort of baby he must have been: a quiet, serious baby who didn't cry very often, who kept his troubles to himself but wanted, more than anything, to be picked up and held.

"Do you still have the matches?"

Walter stopped.

"The matches that told you when to go to the park?"

He walked to his dresser, opened a drawer, and took out a pile of white envelopes.

"Georgina was wrong," he said, handing the pile to Poco. "Sometimes there are three matches, sometimes more. The number isn't important."

Poco spread the envelopes out on the bed beside Walter's other treasures. There were six, five with stamps and one without. Each envelope was addressed to Walter, care of Mrs. Fred Docker, just like Walter's other message from the Match Girl. Poco recognized the same nervous, scratchy writing. The stamps were ordinary. Their postmark dates showed no particular pattern, though Poco saw how the first letters had come close together. The final two had arrived further apart, the last dated over a week ago.

She picked up the unstamped envelope, which had no postmark. "When did this come?"

"It was first," Walter said. "I found it in the mail basket just after Georgina came here. I thought for a while she'd left it to trick me."

"I remember that day. It was a Sunday. We

went to the park and the sandwich shop and everywhere looking for you. Then, on the way home, I ran into my robin. Did I tell you? He's perfectly all right and hangs around my backyard talking to Juliette. No one can believe it, but I think they've made friends."

There was silence while Poco concentrated on the envelopes again. She shifted some around, and picked up the rattle. "Sunday," she murmured, then got to her feet and gazed at Walter.

"Have you ever wondered . . .," she began, and paused to get his attention.

"Walter?" His pale eyes came up to meet hers. "Have you ever wondered if your mother was still alive?"

"Alive? Oh no, she couldn't be," Walter said. "If she were, I would never have been left to stay with Granny."

ELEVEN

GEORGINA WAS, if possible, more impressed by Walter's treasures than Poco. Far from laughing, she picked up every one and examined it with a microscopic eye. The friends were all gathered in Poco's room the next afternoon. Somehow Poco had persuaded Walter to come. He stood by nervously rattling a paper bag, as if he might, at any moment, take his things and leave.

"Beautiful!" Georgina whispered over the locket. "Amazing!" The hospital bracelet disappeared inside her hand. Walter watched closely until she put it down.

Next she alighted upon the socks and the doll-size sweater. Walter sucked in his breath and waited for her to snicker. But she examined them as seriously as the others.

"I guess someone has found out who Walter is."

Walter nodded. "My mother. She knows I need to have these. George, promise you won't tell? I don't want anyone hearing at school."

"Of course not!" Georgina's voice took on commanding tones. "We will proceed in the strictest confidence. You know how the police keep evidence secret."

"Evidence?" Walter glanced up in alarm.

"Well, yes. When we start our investigation . . ."

"Investigation! For what?"

"For finding out who is behind the Little Match Girl," Poco told him. "It's what you've been wanting to know all this time."

Georgina added her vigorous nod. "Even you must admit that it's starting to look as if a real person is doing this. And that's a very good sign because . . ."

"A real person?" Walter cried. "What does that mean?"

"It means not a ghost, or one of your old spir-its!" Georgina had begun to lose her patience.

"A real person is someone we can handle," Poco explained. "We can make a real plan to find out who it is."

"Or even who *she* is," Georgina said. "Because who else but a mother would keep all this stuff?"

For one moment Walter's eyes showed pure fright on their pale surfaces. Then he pulled his cap down and hid them from view. "No plans," he said. "I don't want any plans."

"But why?" Poco and Georgina couldn't believe it. "Don't you want to know?"

"No."

"Walter! Why?"

He would not answer. "I'm going home," he announced, and put his treasures into the bag. "I need to see if there were any messages today. They've been coming slower, and I'm beginning to think . . . "

"Walter, wait!" Georgina and Poco followed him outside, stepping squarely on Juliette, who was asleep on the mat.

"I'm beginning to think there might not be many more. So please don't come to see the Match Girl,"

Walter told them as he went down the walk. "It's very important. She must be left alone."

"You can't order us to do that!" Georgina cried. "The Match Girl belongs to us as much as you."

Poco ran after him. "And what about the flowers . . . ?"

"Stay away!" Walter shrieked in a strange, wild voice. "Stay away or you'll end up wrecking everything."

NEVER HAD Walter Kew acted so rude and crazy. After he rushed off, Poco and Georgina stared at each other, and then at Juliette, who had retreated to a corner of the porch to lick her wounds.

There seemed no earthly reason why the same Walter who had longed for his mother and waited for her voice and tried to contact her in every possible way would now, suddenly, call off the search.

"Just when we were getting close." Poco clenched her fist. "When I think about the locket and those little socks . . . Someone kept those things for years because they cared about Walter. Someone hid those things away because they couldn't forget. Why doesn't he want to know who it is?"

Georgina shook her head. "There's something else. If these things are so precious, why is this mother giving them up? And why leave them one by one in a park?"

They sat down on the porch steps. Juliette came padding over, and their hands were drawn like magnets to her silky back. The sounds of summer wafted in from all directions—baseball, outdoor voices, the screech of bicycle brakes. It was a perfect, lazy June afternoon, except somewhere close by a child was crying.

"I read the story of the Little Match Girl again last night," Georgina said, as they patted the cat. "You know what? I still don't get it. While hundreds of people are walking past, a girl like us quietly freezes? Why doesn't she cry out and ask for help?"

Poco shrugged. "Maybe she's ashamed. She feels bad to be poor. Maybe she thinks it's her fault."

"So she tries to stay warm by lighting her own matches? I would have gone and found a pile of wood."

"I guess she'd already gotten too cold. And

anyway, that's when the magic begins. When-ever she strikes a match, a beautiful picture comes that makes her warm."

"Except she's using up the matches she should have sold. In the end, the Match Girl will be even poorer."

"She knows that, but she can't help it."

"So she lights another match. And then another. One by one by one by one . . ." Georgina's voice turned soft and thoughtful. "For some reason that reminds me of something."

"Walter's treasures!" They both said it at once. It was almost as if the Match Girl herself had spoken and made them understand after all this time. Below, on the step, Juliette stared at them.

Poco jumped to her feet. "Walter's mother *is* alive, and she keeps watch in the park. Then one by one she leaves her treasures."

"And then," said Georgina, "she waits for Walter to come."

"Because she wants to see him. Is that really all?"

"I think she's as scared as Walter. She doesn't dare to go any closer."

"But it's so strange," whispered Poco. "She really is like the Little Match Girl. She uses matches to get Walter to come. Then she can watch him for a while and feel warm and happy. Do you think she knows the Match Girl's story?"

"More than that. Remember how Walter said his presents were coming slower? It's like the matches in the story. She's using them up."

"Oh no! What will happen when there aren't any more?"

"She'll get cold," said Georgina. "She'll get very, very cold."

TWECVE

ONE THING Walter knew: his mother had come to see him. From across her dark ocean she had heard his call, and she had come and brought with her all the memories she could carry. She couldn't speak to him directly, he understood. That went beyond what the dead could do. But by giving him back his own first things, she could tell him the stories of how his family had been—what he had played with, how he had looked, how he was carried and dressed, the ways he was loved. And missed.

Because he was missed, Walter could see that now. His parents hadn't simply disappeared and forgotten. They might have gone to a far-off place. They might have changed, turned to air, lost their bodies and faces. But they had not forgotten. No, not once. They had loved him across sea and time and space.

How terrible it must have been for them to leave him behind. Walter saw how they had worried before they died. Desperately they had made a desperate plan. What else could be the meaning of the big casserole? His mother had found it and packed him up to go. She had wrapped him in a blanket and composed a special note. She had chosen the family that would take him in: older people who had always longed for a baby. She was smart to think of that, and wise to give him in secret. Otherwise his grandparents might not have been allowed to keep him. "Too old," the authorities might have said, or "too poor"—and sent him to live with strangers.

But, best of all, this smart, amazing mother had come when he most needed her. He felt her presence all day as he walked about, and at night when he lay alone in bed—not outside him like a ghost but as an inside happiness. Though soon, of course, she would have to go away. It was the law of the dead: they could not stay. They could come for a little and invisibly watch. They could send presents, enter dreams, conjure up the past. But then, sad as it was, they must go back.

Walter Kew knew all this. He wasn't making a fuss. He just wanted his mother to stay as long as she could. She must not grow tired of him, or be frightened off by his interfering friends. She must be allowed to come and go in the park, to visit the Little Match Girl whenever she liked.

And, especially, she must hold back none of her precious gifts. Walter wanted them all. He needed them: the locket with the mysterious picture of the soldier, the socks, the sweater, the button-on mitten, the rattle, the hospital bracelet that proved his name. He would save them forever, to his final day, because they told him the story he most needed to hear: that he was and always would be a one-and-only child, who was loved and not forgotten, who had never been given away.

THE AFTERNOON was near its end, but the sun was still hot and bright as Poco and Georgina stepped cautiously through the great iron gate of Andersen Park. The hour was late enough, about 6 P.M., for the baby strollers and littlest children to have gone home. Under the Snow Queen's regal stare, the sandbox sat empty. The swings hung motionless, shoulder to shoulder. Away in a field, a noisy group of boys was choosing up sides for a baseball game.

"Is Walter there?" Georgina asked. Poco's keen eyes focused.

"No."

On her knoll the Match Girl sat alone. She was easier to see now that the weeds and bushes were gone. The shape of her head stood out cleanly in her new alcove, though the slope leading up was as overgrown as ever. Its wild disorder somehow set her further apart. Like a wish or a dream, she floated over the park.

"Okay, let's go." Georgina led off.

They walked past the pond, circling around the knoll to be sure he wasn't there after all, crouched into some nook in his Walter-ish way. But he wasn't. The coast was clear. Boldly they approached, slogging up through the long grass. They came to the statue and gazed about. The wildflower clumps looked brighter and thicker.

"I guess he's been watering," Georgina said.

The Match Girl's small lawn had grown ragged, though, and they had brought nothing along to trim it. A week had passed since they had dared to visit. On this, their first day of summer vacation, they had been waiting since early morning to come. The last thing they wanted was to run into Walter.

Georgina eyed the Match Girl's pockets. "I wonder if he's gotten anything else."

"Nothing lately. I asked him yesterday at school. It's been more than two weeks since the last message."

"Good grief! What does he think is going on? You get him to talk a lot better than I can."

"He thinks the same thing he always has. His parents are dead, but his ghost-mother has come and is watching him. He told me she'll be leaving soon because she has to go back to the dead world."

Georgina shivered. "It's awful. Why does he want to believe that?"

"I don't know."

"And where is his real mother? I am so mad at her. She should stop being scared and come out and talk. Can't she see how she's tearing him up? I think she is a mother who only cares about herself."

"She's around here somewhere. Otherwise, she couldn't watch."

"But where?" Georgina glared out at the park. Starting with the front gate, she turned herself slowly all the way around, looking for possible hiding places.

"Nothing! Just nothing." She stamped off.

Poco sat down near the Little Match Girl and picked at the grass. Suddenly she leaned forward and touched the statue's hand.

"George! Her golden ring is gone."

Georgina came rushing over. The Match Girl's finger was bare. Not only that, but there was no sign of where the ring had been. If they had not known better, they might have thought they had imagined it.

Georgina snorted. "Someone was here."

"But how did they get it off?"

"With a saw, probably. It was worth some money."

Poco gazed about. The area around the statue had been dense with brush. Now, after their work, the knoll was nearly clear, leaving the shy

Match Girl open to the world. Had someone taken advantage of her?

Poco examined her slender bronze hand again but could not see a single cut or scratch. The ring had been removed without any trace of force.

She was gazing out at the park again when a wind she knew well blew across her cheek. The eyes of the watcher were on her again, cool, steady, and invisible. Was it Walter's mother? A flash of light erupted near the park entrance. Poco caught her breath, but it was only the sun, its lowering rays reflected off some bright surface—a bicycler's mirror or a passing car. A moment later, she saw exactly what it was: the front window of the sandwich shop across the street.

Flash! The window went off again. Flash! It ignited with a golden glow. A person might suppose that, behind the glass, someone was desperately trying to signal. But soon the sun began to move on. The store darkened, then receded into shadow. Except—what was that? Poco rose to her feet. Where the golden glow had been, she saw the outline of a face.

"Georgina! Georgina! I know where she's hiding."

"Where?"

"In the sandwich shop."

"The sandwich shop! You can't even see it from here."

"Yes, you can. Look! Through the park gate. Walter's mother is there watching us, I think."

"But no one's ever in there now, except that poor waitress. . . ."

Georgina's eyes widened. Poco's tiny hands flew to her mouth.

"The waitress!" They whispered it to each other.

A second later, the Match Girl was left behind, and they were running wildly across the park.

SHE WAS IN THERE. Through the window they saw her long, thin shape behind the sandwich shop's counter. They stood directly across the street, catching their breaths.

The store had fallen into late afternoon shadow. Indoor lights faintly brightened the room. They saw her step up to put something on a shelf. She came down, turned her back, bent over, then straightened. She was washing things, with the same quick movements their own mothers made at home. She washed a pot and cocked it upside down to dry. With a dish towel she polished some plates and stacked them. She wiped off the counter and rinsed the sponge under a faucet. She looked ordinary and never once glanced out the window.

"Are you sure it's her?" Georgina said.

For an answer, Poco crossed the street. She opened the sandwich shop's door and went inside. Georgina scuttled in behind her.

"Yes? Can I help you?" The waitress spotted them. She came forward, peering through fallen wisps of hair that she pushed aside with a hot, impatient hand. Her face was flushed. She looked suddenly rather young.

"Hello. We'd like some sodas," Poco invented. "What kind did you say you wanted, George?"

"Um . . . ah . . ." Georgina looked pale.

"Orange? Okay. Two orange sodas, please." Poco stared boldly at the waitress. In the photo, Walter's mother's hair had been dark. This woman's was light brown, and shorter.

They sat at one of the little café tables. She waited on them the same way she had before, without giving any sign of recognition. Perhaps all children looked the same to her? Poco had found it often true of adults. They seemed to be forever mixing her up with others.

The waitress brought them napkins, straws, and the sodas.

"Thank you."

"You're welcome." She had brown eyes and a pretty, sloping nose. Nothing except her slightness reminded Poco of Walter. Could she once have had a child? She seemed more like someone's older sister.

Georgina kept glancing around. The grumpy shop owner was not in sight, but through the swinging doors came the sound of crashing pots.

The waitress went to stand behind the meat counter. She leaned her hip against the sink and stared out the window.

Poco took a breath and raised her voice. "Have you seen Walter today?"

The waitress's face came around quickly. "Sorry, were you speaking to me?"

"Yes. You know, our friend. The skinny boy in the baseball cap?"

She gazed at them for a long moment.

"Oh, that one." She looked away. "Yes, I see him, but not so often these days."

"You know he lives with his grandmother," Poco said. "That's because both his parents are dead."

"Dead?" Her voice came back like an echo.

"When he was a baby, they had an accident."

"That's sad." She stared straight at Poco.

Poco looked at her in silence. Was this the sort of person who would leave a baby at someone's door, who would keep his things like treasures and then use them as a lure? Had she loved a soldier? Would she send matchsticks through the mail? Could she hide, time after time, when her child walked by? If only one could see into her secret mind.

The waitress moved around and clinked some glasses. She glanced at her watch.

"Do you want another soda?" she asked. "We're getting ready to close."

They got up and paid—with Georgina's money. She was staring too hard at the waitress to protest.

"Could you tell us how much tip we're supposed to leave?" Poco asked the woman. "We haven't done it by ourselves before." It was the last thing she could think of to keep the conversation going. Georgina glared and looked embarrassed.

The waitress smiled. "That's very nice, but you weren't any trouble."

"But we'd like to. It's what's fair."

"Well, for two sodas, you could leave a quarter."

Georgina fished another quarter out of her wallet and walked over and laid it reluctantly on the table. But even this wasn't enough for Poco, who insisted on picking the quarter up and delivering it personally to the waitress's hand.

"Thank you," the waitress said. Her eyes darted up. "Aren't you the girl who worries about squirrels?"

"That's right."

"I'm sorry I didn't recognize you sooner. Please say hello to your friend from me. The skinny one—what's his name again?"

"Walter Kew."

"Yes. He's a nice kid." The waitress's eyes rested softly on Poco. Then she turned and began to shut off the shop's lights.

"Well," said Georgina, as they walked away

down the sidewalk. "It wasn't her at all. She hardly even knew us. She didn't really care about a person named Walter. It didn't matter to her whether his parents were dead or alive. All she wanted was to get off work."

Poco frowned and shook her head. "Did you notice her hand?"

"Kind of red—from washing all those dishes, I guess."

"Georgina, she was wearing the Match Girl's ring. I saw it on her finger when she took the quarter."

THIRTEEN

THE PROBLEM was how to tell Walter.

Two days passed while Poco and Georgina tried to think. A mother cannot be simply announced. And if she is changing from dead to alive, from ghost to flesh-colored, everyday woman, a great deal of care needs to be taken. The friends had not really thought of it before, but lost and found mothers can be very difficult.

Walter had a sensitive nature. He might get upset and refuse to listen. He might decide he didn't want a real mother around. After all, he'd spent his life with Granny Docker. What if this mother wanted him to be with her? He'd have to move in with a whole new person.

Georgina said, "We're lucky we already know our mothers and have learned how to live with all the crazy things they do. If we had to meet them now, we probably couldn't stand them."

They were sitting under a tree in Poco's back-yard on a blazing hot afternoon. Juliette lay nearby, flat on her back and all four feet in the air. But she was not quite asleep, because when, from above, a robin's voice sang out, one of her Siamese eyes cracked open.

"Walter will be stubborn," Georgina went on, steeling herself.

"He will tell us to go away and leave him alone."

"He'll be angry, just the way he was before."

"His whole life could change." This thought made them rather breathless. But how could Walter be allowed to go on believing in ghosts? There comes a time when a person must grow up and face the facts.

"We must tell him today," Georgina declared. "We'll call him and ask him to meet us at the park. Then we can explain what we saw in the sandwich shop. He'll probably want to go alone to see his mother."

Poco said, softly, "I hope she wants to see him."

They were just on the point of getting up from the grass when who should appear but . . .

"Walter!"

He came across the yard with a cheerful stride. Juliette sat up at once.

"Hello. And hello, Juliette." He bent over and gave her ears a friendly scratch. "I came to tell you," he said, straightening up, "that everything is back to normal. You can come see the Little Match Girl whenever you want. My mother has left."

"Left!"

"Yes, and I'm sorry I got so mad. I just wanted to be sure she had all the space she needed."

"Space?" The friends gazed at him in alarm.

"To leave me my things. But now she has."

"Wait a minute! How can that be?" Georgina sounded as sharp as a chief of police.

Walter drew a thin box from his pocket. "A message came from the Match Girl in yesterday's mail, and when I went to the park, this is what I found." He took off the box's cover. Inside, on tissue paper, lay a curl of dark brown hair.

"Your mother's?" Georgina leapt back in horror.

Walter laughed. "Of course not. It's a baby's."

"It's yours," Poco said. "Your mother must have cut it just before she gave you up."

"That's right. This is her last treasure. When I found it yesterday, I knew she had gone."

Walter sighed. "My mother was the bravest person. You can't imagine how hard she worked. To be invisible and have to watch, not to be able to reach out and touch—it took all her energy and force. She lasted as long as she possibly could. Someday, who knows, she might come back. She never really told me about my father, though she left some clues. I think he was a soldier."

Poco and Georgina could only stare.

"And my grandmother said his last name might have been Walter, because of the name on my hospital bracelet. Like yours, Poco, remember how you said—"

"Walter, good grief . . . !" Georgina began, and

stopped. He had it all so completely worked out. He loved a mother he'd made up. How could they tell him about the real one?

"Anyway," Walter said, "we can talk about it later. Right now I have a special treat. My grandmother gave me ten dollars and said I should use it on my friends. I think she was afraid they might have given me up."

"You mean us?" Poco said.

"Who else?" Walter's face clouded over. "Unless you don't want to . . ."

"Of course we do! Why do you always have to say that?" Georgina thundered.

Walter smiled with relief. Then, while Juliette looked on with approving eyes, he issued a startling invitation. He would like it so much if they would come with him now to visit the Little Match Girl. On the way they would stop at the sandwich shop so he could buy them . . . well, whatever they wanted! Sodas, candy, magazines, hot fudge sundaes.

"Because I'm loaded!" he cried, pulling his money out. "And then I'd know for sure we're all back together."

There was no way around it. Walter's mind was set. To suggest any change would have hurt his feelings. He led them eagerly down the street and even insisted on taking Juliette when she staggered to her feet and tried to follow.

"We should put her in the house," Poco objected. Walter wouldn't think of it. The old cat had taken a hold on his feelings.

"Would you like a ride?" he offered her gallantly. Juliette switched her tail and walked ahead. Above her came a rustle of robin wings.

"Go home," Poco told the bird sternly. "And take Juliette. This is none of your business."

But neither paid the least attention, and on they all went in Walter's weird procession.

"Are we going to tell him?" Georgina whispered to Poco.

"We have to."

"But how?"

"I don't know."

The iron gate of Andersen Park rose into view. Georgina stopped to look at the Little Match Girl as they went by. Mysterious and distant she appeared from there, and far removed from all that was happening.

"George! Come on." The procession had arrived. Everyone else was poised outside the sandwich shop door. Walter stood in the lead like a proud general. They waited for Georgina to cross the street, then all went in—except for Poco's robin. He settled down in a nearby tree. With his craning neck and shiny black eyes, he looked just as excited as anyone else. Would Walter's mother dare to come out in the open?

Inside, Poco and Georgina squinted and had a first wave of doubt. Behind the shop's counter stood another woman.

"CAN I HELP YOU?"

"Yes, we all want to order." Walter swept his guests forward to a table. Never had he seemed so pleased with himself.

"That cat is not allowed in here." The waitress spoke as they sat down. She was large, middle-aged, and prickly looking. "Animals of any kind are against the law."

"I'll keep her on my lap," Walter promised. He tucked his knees and Juliette under the table. "See? No one will even notice."

"The law is the law. Absolutely no cats!"

"But we can't put her out on the street alone."

"Why not?"

"We just can't!"

114 :

"In that case, out you go." The woman placed threatening hands on her hips.

At this, Juliette herself stood up and gazed at the waitress from Walter's lap. In the sun her blue eyes blazed up like sapphires.

"What is she, a Siamese?" The waitress's voice sounded suddenly nicer. She stepped close and offered her hand. "You certainly are a fascinating thing."

The old cat smiled and gave her a wink.

"Well! I guess . . . I guess she could stay. Who could possibly mind? She is such a beauty." A look of surprise went over the waitress's face, as if she had not expected to say this. Then she shrugged and asked to take their orders. Two hot fudge sundaes. One orange soda. Juliette lay back and began to lick a paw. Georgina stared at her in horror.

"Did you see that?" she whispered to Poco.

But Poco was thinking of something else.

"Where is the other waitress?" she asked the older woman.

"There isn't one, dear. Just me, that's all. We run the place together, me and my husband. There he is standing behind the meat counter."

When they turned, they saw the mean-faced old man eyeing them.

"But someone else was here whenever we came before."

"That part-time girl? We got rid of her. She was supposed to wash dishes and keep the place clean. But there, every time our backs were turned, she'd be doing what she shouldn't—gabbing to folks, writing letters, staring out the window as if her life depended on it."

"But when did she leave?" Georgina couldn't believe it.

"Yesterday morning. We gave her notice a week ago. She didn't mind much. She said she had to go home."

"Home!" Poco glanced at Georgina. "Where was her home, did she ever mention?"

The waitress shrugged and shook her head. "Who knows? Who cares? Not around here any-way. The one time I asked her, she said, 'Across an ocean.'"

FOURTEEN

I T W A S A S I F a door had slammed shut. Poco and Georgina had never felt such a jolt. One minute Walter's mother was there, with a face and a life, and her terrible shyness. The next she was gone—whisk!—out of the world.

"But she was alive. We saw her. She spoke to us!" Georgina said it often in the days following.

"Maybe not," Poco would answer. "That was only what she seemed. She might really have been the ghost-mother Walter believed in. Don't look so upset. These things happen."

"No they don't!" Georgina gave a violent, disbelieving shiver. "Remember how we sat drinking our sodas? She was washing dishes like an ordinary mother. All that time she was really dead?"

Poco smiled. "I think Walter liked her better that way."

"But that has nothing to do with it."

"Maybe it does if you're desperate enough."

About none of this did they ever speak to Walter. What was the use when nothing could be proved? His view of things was as good as theirs. Better, in fact; he was a steadier person. His mother had left him, but this time it was expected. She had done what he had asked, held up her end. For some reason, this gave Walter confidence. There was no need to creep into corners or vanish like Houdini when he felt unsure. Walter walked in the open air. The old demon spirits that had stalked him went away, and he began to take charge of his powerful antennae. Where before they had picked up cold, distant worlds, now his radar worked on things close to home. He saw, for instance, how lonely Granny

Docker was and began to talk to her in a different way.

"Louder, you mean?" Georgina demanded.

"Softer," Walter said. "She hears me better."

Amid all this change and the scurry of summer, the one forgotten thing was the Little Match Girl. The friends never did walk over that morning, because Juliette was struck by a bad case of weakness. Perhaps she had used too much strength on the waitress. Walter was forced to carry her home from the shop, with Poco's robin fluttering wildly overhead. For a while they were afraid the cat would decide to pass on to her next life that very night. But thankfully she rallied and paid them all the compliment of choosing to stay a little longer.

So it was not until nearly the middle of August that the friends found themselves walking up the knoll again, and coming face-to-face with the bronze girl. Juliette, who was with them, thanks to Walter, sat on the little lawn and gazed up at her with a look of grave respect. By now the grass had become quite long. From everywhere bushes seemed to have exploded, and there was a general thickening of stem and foliage. It was amazing to see how fast things could grow. The green veil that had hidden the statue from the park was rising again. Before the month was out, the Little Match Girl would once more crouch in shadow.

At first Poco and Georgina were shocked by this state of neglect. While Walter and Juliette watched, they rushed about, pulling up weeds and vines. But soon the heat of the day overwhelmed them. They lay back on their elbows and gazed out at the park, knowing they would never be able to keep up with nature. The knoll was too wild; its roots went too deep. Even the flowers they had planted were in danger of being choked.

"All that work for nothing," Georgina said.

"Oh no," said Walter. "I don't think that at all. It was nice to see the Match Girl out in the open. Now she wants to go back undercover."

"She wants to!" said Georgina. "How do you know?"

"See how she's trying to turn her face?"

They looked, and it did seem to be so, whether because of the new burst of leaves or a certain cast of afternoon light. Where the Match Girl had appeared to reach out to them before, now she was modestly drawing away.

Suddenly it seemed to them that they'd never really known her. She was a statue from a story that had happened too long ago. They could come to visit her over and over, but they would never understand why she'd frozen as she had. Or whether in the end she was sad, or happy, or if heaven was a place she really wanted to go.

While everyone was thinking these thoughts, Juliette stood up, stretched, and padded toward the statue. She swirled with elegant steps around the Match Girl's hand. Otherwise, Georgina's eye never would have caught it.

"Poco! Walter! Look, a ring!"

It was different from the other. Smoother, plainer, silvery colored.

"Wait a minute!" cried Georgina. "What is going on?"

Walter smiled. "Maybe the Match Girl is expecting another ghost."